Goodbye to Goldie

by Fran Manushkin

illustrated by Tammie Lyon

Picture Window Books
Minneapolis, Minnesota

Katie Woo is published by Picture Window Books
A Capstone Imprint
1710 Roe Crest Drive
North Mankato, MN 56003
www.capstonepub.com

Text © 2010 Fran Manushkin
Illustrations © 2010 Picture Window Books

Library of Congress Cataloging-in-Publication Data
Manushkin, Fran.
    Goodbye to Goldie / by Fran Manushkin; illustrated by Tammie Lyon.
    p. cm. — (Katie Woo)
    ISBN 978-1-4048-5495-6 (library binding)
    ISBN 978-1-4048-6057-5 (softcover)
    [1. Death—Fiction. 2. Grief—Fiction. 3. Dogs—Fiction. 4. Chinese Americans—Fiction.]
I. Lyon, Tammie, ill. II. Title.

    PZ7.M3195Go 2010

    [E]—dc22   2009002188

Summary: Katie Woo learns different ways to cope with the death of her dog.

Creative Director: Heather Kindseth
Graphic Designer: Emily Harris

Photo Credits
Fran Manushkin, pg. 26
Tammie Lyon, pg. 26

Printed in the United States of America in North Mankato, Minnesota.
062017
010595R

✿ Table of Contents ✿

Chapter 1
A Great Dog

Katie Woo's dog, Goldie,

was very old.

DISCARD

One day,

Goldie became

very sick. A week

later, she died.

Katie's mom

held Katie while

she cried.

"I will miss Goldie so much," Katie cried. "She was my best friend."

Katie's friend JoJo hugged
her. "I will miss Goldie too,"
said JoJo. "She was the nicest
dog in the world."

"She was!" agreed Pedro.

"Goldie loved running on the beach," said Pedro.

"We didn't have to go into the sea to get wet," said JoJo. "Goldie would just shake her fur and make us all wet!"

"Goldie was great in the snow, too!" said Pedro. "We used to toss snowballs, and she would try to catch them in her mouth."

Chapter 2
A Wagging Tail

"Tell me some more

happy stories about Goldie,"

said Katie.

JoJo grinned. "That's easy!

There are so many."

"At Thanksgiving, Goldie ate my drumstick," JoJo said. "I turned around, and it was gone!"

"Goldie was smart," said Katie. "And fast!"

"Goldie was so much fun

on Halloween," said Katie.

"Remember the time she

wore a skunk costume? She

ran around and scared all

the other dogs!"

"Goldie loved tickling my face with her tail," said JoJo.

"She dusted the table with it too," joked Katie's mom.

"And my computer!" added Katie's dad.

"Her tail hardly ever

stopped wagging," said Katie.

"Goldie and I
were both scared
of thunder," said
Katie. "But when
we hugged, we both
felt better."

"Goldie was a good cuddler,"
agreed Katie's mom.

Katie's dad showed her

a photo. It was taken when

she and Goldie were little.

They were eating hot dogs

together.

"This photo is great,"

Katie said. "I love looking

at it."

Chapter 3

The **Scrapbook**

JoJo had an idea. "We should make Katie a Goldie scrapbook. She can look at it whenever she feels sad."

Katie's mom found two photos of Goldie and Katie. In one, they were playing catch with a ball.

In the other, they were both very small. They were taking a nap on the grass.

Katie drew a picture of

Goldie catching popcorn in

her mouth.

"She was good at that!"

Katie said, smiling. "She

never missed!"

"Goldie could jump rope too," said JoJo. "And kick a soccer ball!"

"And almost catch squirrels!" added Pedro.

Chasing Squirrels

"Goldie lived a long and

happy life," said Katie's mom.

"She sure did," said Katie.

That night at
bedtime, Katie
held Goldie's
picture and kissed it
good night.

"Goldie, I will always remember you," Katie promised.

And she always did.

About the Author

Fran Manushkin is the author of many popular picture books, including *How Mama Brought the Spring; Baby, Come Out!; Latkes and Applesauce: A Hanukkah Story;* and *The Tushy Book.* There is a real Katie Woo — she's Fran's great-niece — but she never gets in half the trouble of the Katie Woo in the books. Fran writes on her beloved Mac computer in New York City, without the help of her two naughty cats, Cookie and Goldy.

About the Illustrator

Tammie Lyon began her love for drawing at a young age while sitting at the kitchen table with her dad. She continued her love of art and eventually attended the Columbus College of Art and Design, where she earned a bachelors degree in fine art. After a brief career as a professional ballet dancer, she decided to devote herself full time to illustration. Today she lives with her husband, Lee, in Cincinnati, Ohio. Her dogs, Gus and Dudley, keep her company as she works in her studio.

❁ Glossary ❁

computer (kuhm-PYOO-tur)—a machine that can store large amounts of information

costume (KOSS-toom)—clothes worn to look like someone or something else

cuddler (CUD-duhl-lur)—someone who lies next to another person for comfort

photo (FOH-toh)—a picture taken by a camera

scrapbook (SCRAP-buk)—a book with blank pages that hold pictures and other items you wish to keep

thunder (THUHN-dur)—the loud, booming sound that comes after a flash of lightening

❀ Discussion Questions ❀

1. Have you ever had to tell someone goodbye? How did you feel?

2. The book lists many things Goldie liked to do. What other things do dogs like to do?

3. If you could have any kind of pet, what kind of pet would you choose?

✿ Writing Prompts ✿

1. Goldie was Katie's best friend. What sort of things do you do with your friends? Make a list.

2. Goldie dressed up like a skunk for Halloween. Think of another costume for Goldie and draw a picture of her in it. Write a sentence to explain why it would make a good costume for Goldie.

3. Katie remembers Goldie with a scrapbook. Another way to remember something is to write about it in a journal. Start your own journal, and write about something you want to remember.

Having Fun
with
Katie Woo

In *Goodbye to Goldie*, Katie and her friends make a scrapbook that is all about her dog, Goldie. Make your own scrapbook page. Here's how:

1. Gather your supplies

You will need a piece of paper, crayons, markers, a glue stick, photos, stickers, and anything else you want to use to decorate your page. Any type of paper will work, but if you want your page to last forever, ask an adult for acid-free paper.

2. Choose a theme

What will your page be about? A grandparent, a favorite book, or a family vacation all make fun themes.

3. Get to work

Choose which photos you want to include. Do you want to include captions to describe your photos? What about some stickers? Before you glue anything down, lay your items out on your page to see how they fit. Then use your glue to stick them down.

Once your page is finished you can put it in an album. Then you can add more pages and build a whole scrapbook. Or treat your page as a work of art, and hang it up for all to see!